28 FEB 2002   09 DEC 2014

D1341761

For Sharmon, Nathene and Christine

1 3 5 7 9 10 8 6 4 2

© Jane Hissey 2001

Jane Hissey has asserted her right under
the Copyright, Designs and Patents Act, 1988,
to be identified as the author and illustrator of this work

First published in the United Kingdom in 2001 by
Hutchinson Children's Books
The Random House Group Limited
20 Vauxhall Bridge Road, London SW1V 2SA

Random House Australia (Pty) Limited
20 Alfred Street, Milsons Point, Sydney
New South Wales 2061, Australia

Random House New Zealand Limited
18 Poland Road, Glenfield
Auckland 10, New Zealand

Random House South Africa (Pty) Limited
Endulini, 5A Jubilee Road, Parktown 2193, South Africa

The Random House Group Limited Reg. No. 954009

www.randomhouse.co.uk

A CIP catalogue record for this book
is available from the British Library

ISBN: 0 09 176957 4

Printed in Singapore

Old Bear's
All-Together
Painting

JANE HISSEY

HUTCHINSON
London Sydney Auckland Johannesburg

Old Bear had been busy all afternoon painting a picture.
'I found this tiny frame,' he told
the other toys. 'My painting of
Little Bear will just fit in nicely.'

'I want to
paint a picture
too,' said Little Bear. 'Are there any more frames?'
   'There's a big one,' said Old Bear. 'Why don't you
all paint a picture together. That would be fun.'

'I want to do my *own* painting,' said Little Bear,
'all by myself.'
  'So do I,' said Rabbit.
  'And me,'
barked Ruff.

'Old Bear could choose one to go in the big frame,'
said Jolly Tall.

  'But what shall we paint?' asked Duck. 'We can't
all do pictures of Little Bear.'

  'I don't see why not,' said Little Bear.

'I think I'll paint a ball,' said Ruff, 'or a spaceship or maybe a house . . .'

'Or just a pattern,' suggested Little Bear.

'Why don't we *all* do patterns?' said Rabbit. 'I think I'll paint stripes.'

He dipped two brushes in the paint and bounced along the paper, painting lines as he went.

'Oh dear!' he sighed when he reached the end. 'My stripes are all wavy.'

'That's because you bounce up and down, up and down when you run,' laughed Bramwell Brown.

Meanwhile Jolly had painted a row of orange dots.
'This is my spotty pattern,' he said proudly.

But the paint was much too runny. The toys watched as
it dribbled all the way down to the bottom of the paper.
   'Your spots have turned into stripes,' said Duck.
   'And they're straighter stripes than mine,' said Rabbit.

Little Bear was waving his paint brush above his head.

'Look,' he cried, 'I can make hundreds of spots.
My paper is covered in them.'

'And so are you,' laughed the other toys.

'I'm doing GIANT spots,'
barked Ruff.
    He bounced his rubber ball
into the paint pot, then onto the paper.
    SPLODGE!
    It made a big splattered blob of yellow.

'That's fun,' cried Little Bear. 'Do it again.'
   But this time the ball missed the paper and landed
SPLASH in the water.

'Oh, Ruff,' cried Duck, 'now there are puddles all over my painting.'

'Sorry,' said Ruff, dabbing the splashes with a cloth. 'Is that better?'

'It isn't quite the pattern I wanted,' grumbled Duck.

'It's lovely!' said Old Bear, as he arrived to collect the paintings. 'In fact, all your patterns are perfect.'

'I don't think so,' said Duck, staring at the dribbles and splodges and wiggly lines.

'Just wait and see,' called Old Bear, as he hurried away.

The toys were still clearing away the painting things when Old Bear returned a little later.

'Now cover your eyes and come with me,' he said, 'and no peeping till we're there!'

Old Bear led the toys to a large picture propped against
the wall. 'Now you can look,' he said.

They all stared in amazement.
'Oh, its lovely,' cried
Little Bear. 'Who did it?'

'You all did,' laughed Old Bear. 'I just cut out your patterns and stuck them together. Look, Jolly's orange stripes are the boat and Rabbit's wavy lines are the sea.'

'So Ruff's yellow splodge is the sun,' said Duck, 'and I must have painted the sky.'

'I can see my spots,' cried Little Bear, 'on the sails of the boat.'

'That's right,' said Old Bear, 'and you all did the patterns on the fish.'

'I see,' said Little Bear. 'So we did do an
all-together painting after all. That was fun!'
'I said it would be,' laughed Old Bear.

'And now, after all
our hard work,
let's have an
all-together tea!'

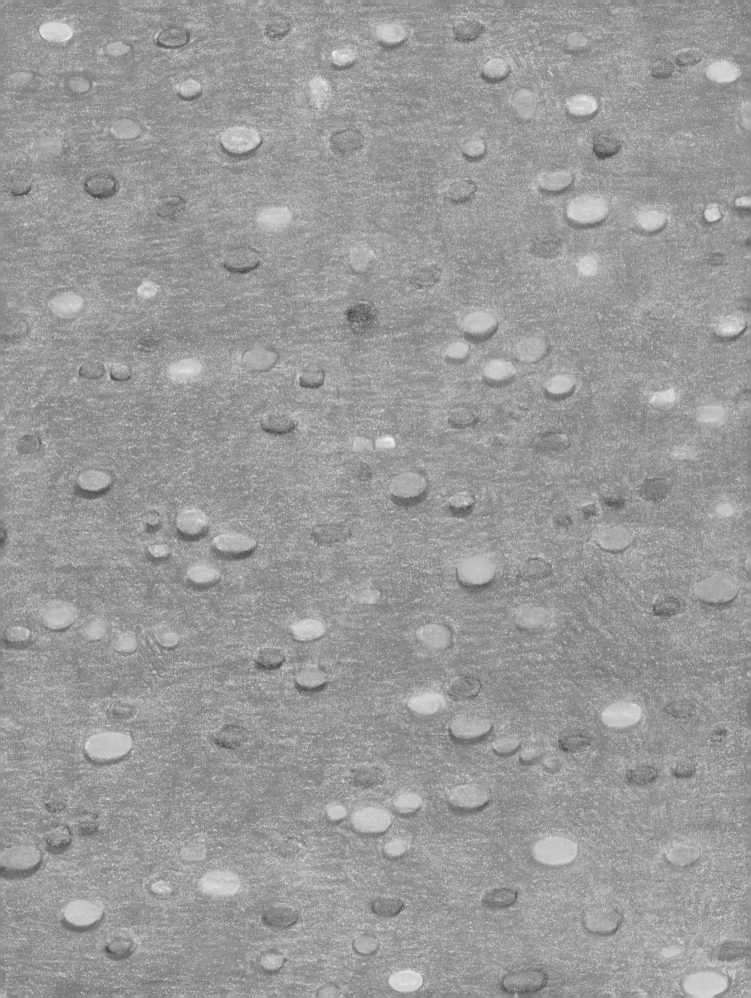